For Edite Kroll

Library of Congress Control Number: 2016950350

ISBN 978-0-06-249431-3

The artist used charcoal sketches painted digitally to create the illustrations for this book.

Typography by Dana Fritts and Andrea Vandergrift

17 18 19 20 21 SCP 10 9 8 7 6 5 4 3 2 1

❖ First Edition

WHAT THIS STORY NEEDS IS

A VROOM AND A ZOOM

By Emma J. Virján

HARPER
An Imprint of HarperCollinsPublishers

W hat this story needs is
a pig in a wig,

rushing to her car,

dashing into place,

ready to start the
cross-country race.

This story also needs a flap,

a squeal,

a rooaarr,

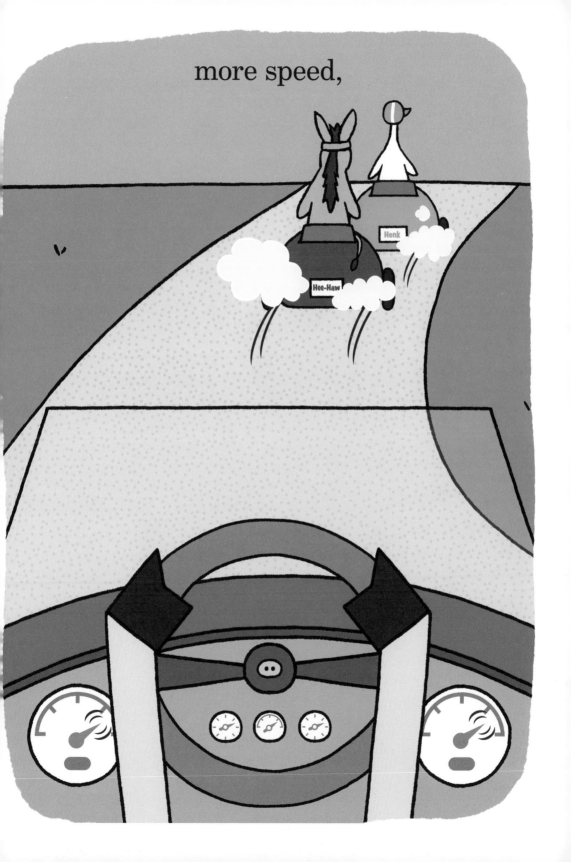

a pig in a wig
taking the lead,

a rumble,

a spin,

a thud,

a plop, and a hisssss,

a car in the mud,

a lift, a spare,

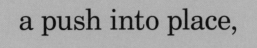

a push into place,

and a pig in a wig
back in the race!

What this story needs is
a vroom,

a zoom,

and a wheeeeee,

What this story needs now is . . .

a victory lap!